Published by Scholastic Australia in 2024.

Scholastic Australia Pty Limited
PO Box 579 Gosford NSW 2250
ABN 11 000 614 577
www.scholastic.com.au

Part of the Scholastic Group
Sydney • Auckland • New York • Toronto • London • Mexico City
New Delhi • Hong Kong • Buenos Aires • Puerto Rico

ISBN 978-1-76152-817-0

Printed in China.

Scholastic Australia's policy, in association with its printers, is to use papers that are renewable and made efficiently from wood grown in responsibly managed forests, so as to minimise its environmental footprint.

Royals and Villains

Adapted by Kristy Boyce
Based on the films by Josann McGibbon & Sara Parriott
and Dan Frey & Russell Sommer

SCHOLASTIC
SYDNEY AUCKLAND NEW YORK TORONTO LONDON MEXICO CITY
NEW DELHI HONG KONG BUENOS AIRES PUERTO RICO

Agrabah
The Great Wall of Auradon
Northern Wei
Lone Keep
Triton's Bay
Camelot
Heights
Sherwood
Forest
Enchanted
Lake
Charmington
Cinderellasburg
Isle of the Lost
N
E
W
S

THE FOUNDING OF

AURADON

Before the creation
of the United States of Auradon, this land was divided into many different kingdoms.

Among them were these:

- Agrabah
- Auradon City
- Auroria
- Bayou De Orleans
- Camelot Heights
- Charmington
- Cinderellasburg
- Mount Olympus
- Northern Wei
- Tangletown
- Wonderland

Each kingdom was ruled separately,
and people with villainous intentions lived side by side with innocent citizens. Instead of protecting one another, the kingdoms protected only themselves—and because of this, there was no peace in the land soon to become **Auradon**.

After marrying, Beast and Belle spent their honeymoon joining the fairy-tale kingdoms together into the United States of Auradon. They ruled this new kingdom as king and queen, striving to give their citizens peace and prosperity. However, not every kingdom joined the USA. The Queen of Hearts, ruler of Wonderland, decided she didn't want her kingdom united with the others.

In one of Beast's first royal decrees as king, he announced that magic would be restricted in Auradon. Beast knew firsthand how dangerous magic could be, having been cursed as a young man, and he wanted the people of Auradon to be free to focus on their interests and talents without magic getting in the way.

THE CREATION OF THE ISLE OF THE LOST

To bring peace to the United States of Auradon, Beast gathered all the villains and their families and sent them to the Isle of the Lost. Fairy Godmother created a magical barrier to keep them from escaping. There was no magic on the Isle, either, and the villains and Villain Kids (VKs) had to fend for themselves to survive.

AURADON TRADITIONS

Auradon became a land of many traditions—from small daily habits to kingdom-wide ceremonies.

One of the biggest celebrations in Auradon is the coronation of the king, which occurred for the first time when Beast and Belle were crowned as king and queen of the United States of Auradon. A coronation takes place at Auradon Cathedral, and all the heroes and royals from around Auradon are invited—which means it's also a huge fashion moment for the kingdom.

Of course, a coronation doesn't always go perfectly, no matter how much planning is involved. During Ben's coronation, Maleficent turned up and tried to overthrow his family as rulers of the kingdom! Mal had to battle her mother and ended up turning her into a lizard. She saved all of Auradon, and the coronation proceeded smoothly from there.

Located in the heart of Auradon City, Auradon Cathedral is the site of grand celebrations, like King Ben's coronation.

Ben let all of Auradon know he was serious about Mal when he invited her to be his date to his coronation ceremony.

Another beloved tradition in Auradon is the Royal Cotillion. The Cotillion is the official royal gathering at which young women are introduced to the court.

One of the most dramatic Cotillions in Auradon history was when King Ben introduced Mal as a new lady of the court. The event was hosted by Lumiere and took place on the *True Love* yacht in Belle's Harbor. Unbeknownst to the guests—including Mal—her VK nemesis, Uma, had used Mal's notebook to spell Ben into believing he was in love with her instead of Mal. Uma then used her power to command Fairy Godmother to bring down the magical barrier around the Isle of the Lost. Luckily, Mal was able to break off the love spell by kissing Ben. Then she transformed into a dragon to stop Uma from causing any damage.

Ultimately, Uma swam off in her octopus form, and the guests danced the night away while celebrating Ben and Mal. That was certainly a night to remember!

While it may be a good excuse for Auradon's teens to get dressed up, the Royal Cotillion also serves as a formal introduction to the court.

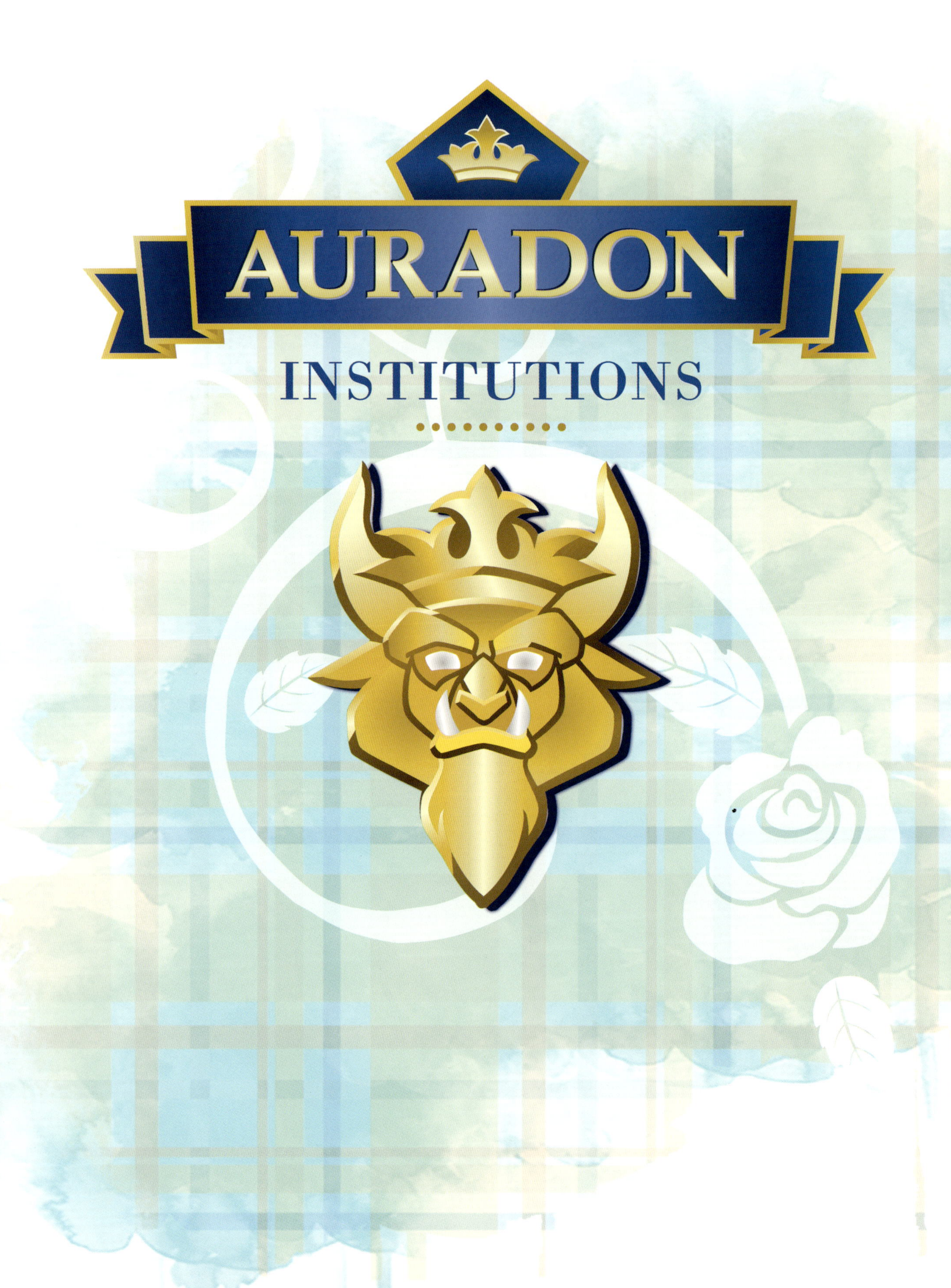
AURADON
INSTITUTIONS

Merlin Academy

Before the fairy-tale kingdoms were united, kids from the regions of Auradon attended Merlin Academy, a school founded and run by the great sorcerer Merlin. The architecture of the school was stunning, with marble details brought in from Camelot and wooden beams from the forests of Auradon.

Because Merlin was headmaster, magic was an important part of the school culture and curriculum. Students took classes in different magical disciplines, from transfiguration to alchemy. You could often find kids practicing spells in the courtyard or their dorm rooms, and magic was also used to keep the school secure.

At Merlin Academy, the children of heroes and villains lived and learned together—and this definitely led to some tricky situations. The kids mostly got along, but fights and bullying between the two groups were common. Some competitions were more good-natured, though. One of the most anticipated events was the annual school dance, Castlecoming. As the event of the year, it had everyone competing to attend with the most stylish outfit and the best date. Castlecoming is still a favorite occasion now that Merlin Academy has become Auradon Prep!

Auradon Prep

After King Beast created the United States of Auradon, Merlin Academy was transformed into Auradon Prep. Some original elements have endured: students still live in dorms together, take classes, participate in extracurriculars, and hang out together at cool events. However, magic is no longer taught in school. Nowadays, most classes are fairly standard—like chemistry and math—but others focus on heroic leadership, dragon anatomy, and life skills without magic. And of course, they teach Remedial Goodness 101 for the new VKs.

There are all kinds of fun extracurriculars to participate in when classes end. One of the most popular is the swords and shields team, which has boasted Jay, Lonnie, and Chad and Chloe Charming as members. Other extracurriculars include tourney, cheerleading, marching band, and the Gadgets and Gizmos tech club.

School at Auradon Prep wouldn't be complete without lots of special events as well. Among others, the school hosts Family Day, Canine Appreciation Day, an annual fashion show (Evie's and Dizzy's favorite!), and monthly dance-offs.

Auradon Prep isn't the only well-known school in the world. Other lands also have their own schools, most notably Dragon Hall on the Isle of the Lost.

The Museum of Cultural History

The Museum of Cultural History is a very important institution in Auradon. When Beast brought the original nineteen fairy-tale kingdoms together, he decreed that citizens would no longer use magic in the United States of Auradon. Instead, all magical objects would be collected and kept in this museum.

Located just two miles from Auradon Prep, the museum has both wards and a guard to protect the valuable magical artifacts—as Mal, Evie, Jay, and Carlos discovered when they broke into the museum! Among the collection are famous items, such as:

- Beast's Enchanted Rose
- Mal's (previously Maleficent's) Spell Book
- Evie's Magic Mirror
- Fairy Godmother's Magic Wand
- Cinderella's Glass Slipper
- Sleeping Beauty's Spinning Wheel
- King Triton's Trident
- Maleficent's Scepter
- Genie of Agrabah's Genie's Lamp

Auradon Prep

THE CITIZENS OF
AURADON

Beast
Belle
Mal
AURADON

Ben

Title: King of the United States of Auradon
Affiliation: Auradon Kid (AK)
Home Kingdom: Auradon City
Family Object: Beast's enchanted rose

Ben's Relationships

Son of Beast and Belle

Husband of Mal

Ben is known as a kind and optimistic king who is a defender of others, including the VKs. Before he became king, he encouraged his parents to bring the VKs to Auradon because he believed they deserved a chance at redemption. Ben kept an open mind and helped them see Auradon as their new home. His favorite VK is his wife, Mal. He fell in love with her and accepted her completely, even when she wasn't sure she was cut out for royal life. He also introduced Carlos and Dude and helped bring down the barrier so that all VKs could have a new life in Auradon.

Belle
Ben
URADON

Beast

Title: Former king of the United States of Auradon
Home Kingdom: Auradon City
Family Object: Enchanted rose

Beast's Relationships

Husband of Belle
Father of Ben

Beast created the United States of Auradon by uniting all nineteen fairy-tale kingdoms. He also banished all villains and their families to the Isle of the Lost and put up a ward to keep them imprisoned there. Beast is confident, strong, and thoughtful, and he's a devoted husband and father. He can also be temperamental and "growly" at times, particularly when the safety of the kingdom is in jeopardy. He wasn't always sure if the choice to bring the VKs to Auradon was the right one, but ultimately, he trusted his son and realized that every kid deserves a chance.

Belle

Title: Former queen of the United States of Auradon
Home Kingdom: Auradon City
Family Object: Beast's enchanted rose

Belle's Relationships

Wife of Beast
Mother of Ben

Belle is an incredibly compassionate and kind person and ruled as queen of Auradon before King Ben ascended the throne. Though her relationship with Beast was rocky at first, they grew close, then got married after Beast's curse was lifted. Since then, they have worked together to rule the United States of Auradon and create a happy and peaceful kingdom. Now that her son is king, Belle hopes to support and advise him while also giving him space to make his own decisions.

Beast
Ben

FATHERS AND SONS

Many children look up to their fathers for their knowledge and wisdom about the world. Ben's relationship with Beast is the perfect example of this. Ben has always admired his father: he watched Beast rule Auradon with benevolence and hoped that he could fill his dad's (very large) shoes when he became king. At the same time, Ben knows his father isn't perfect. Ben believed the villains on the Isle of the Lost deserved a second chance, and he stood by his decision to allow VKs into Auradon even when his father had doubts. Because Ben and Beast have such a strong relationship, they were able to work through those differences. They've always supported each other and continue to do so today.

While not all fathers and sons share a bond like this, some sons still learn important skills from their fathers. Maddox and the Mad Hatter might not be super close, but Maddox definitely got his eccentric creativity and out-of-the-box thinking from his dad. That's what led Maddox to be such an amazing inventor!

Jafar's main goal in life is to collect as much money as possible, in whatever way he can. That has included having his son, Jay, as a "partner" in his junk shop business, but only so Jay could steal items for them to sell. The upside? It taught Jay to be quick and stealthy—skills he used at Auradon Prep to lead his tourney team to victory many times!

Top: King Beast was a noble ruler of the United States of Auradon, but when Ben took over the throne, he had his own ideas about how to rule the kingdom. **Below:** Jafar had hoped he and Jay could work together, but Jay had his own plans.

Jane

Affiliation: Auradon Kid (AK)
Home Kingdom: Auradon City
Family Object: Fairy Godmother's wand

Jane's Relationships

Daughter of Fairy Godmother
Dated Carlos

Jane is a sweet and conscientious girl. She's had times of uncertainty about herself, but her confidence has grown as she's made friends and become closer with the VKs. Jane is very involved with organizing fun events for Auradon Prep.

Fairy Godmother
Carlos

Fay

Also Known As: Fairy Godmother
Home Kingdom: Auradon City
Family Object: Magic wand

When she was a teen, Fay struggled with her magic and questioned her abilities. Though she'd been bequeathed a magic wand, she wasn't a natural when it came to spell work—and it showed. At times she was even bullied by her classmates. Luckily, she found true friends in some of them, like Ella and Bridget.

Before she mastered Bibbidi Bobbidi Boo, a young Fairy Godmother (Fay) was perfecting her craft at Merlin Academy.

WELCOME TO REMEDIAL
Jane
IF SOMEONE
YOU A CRYING
BABY, DO
CURSE IT?
B) LOCK IT IN A
IT A BOTTLE
OUT IT'S
#2- YOU
YOU:
IN THE
ON AN
IT OVER TO
AUTHORITIES?

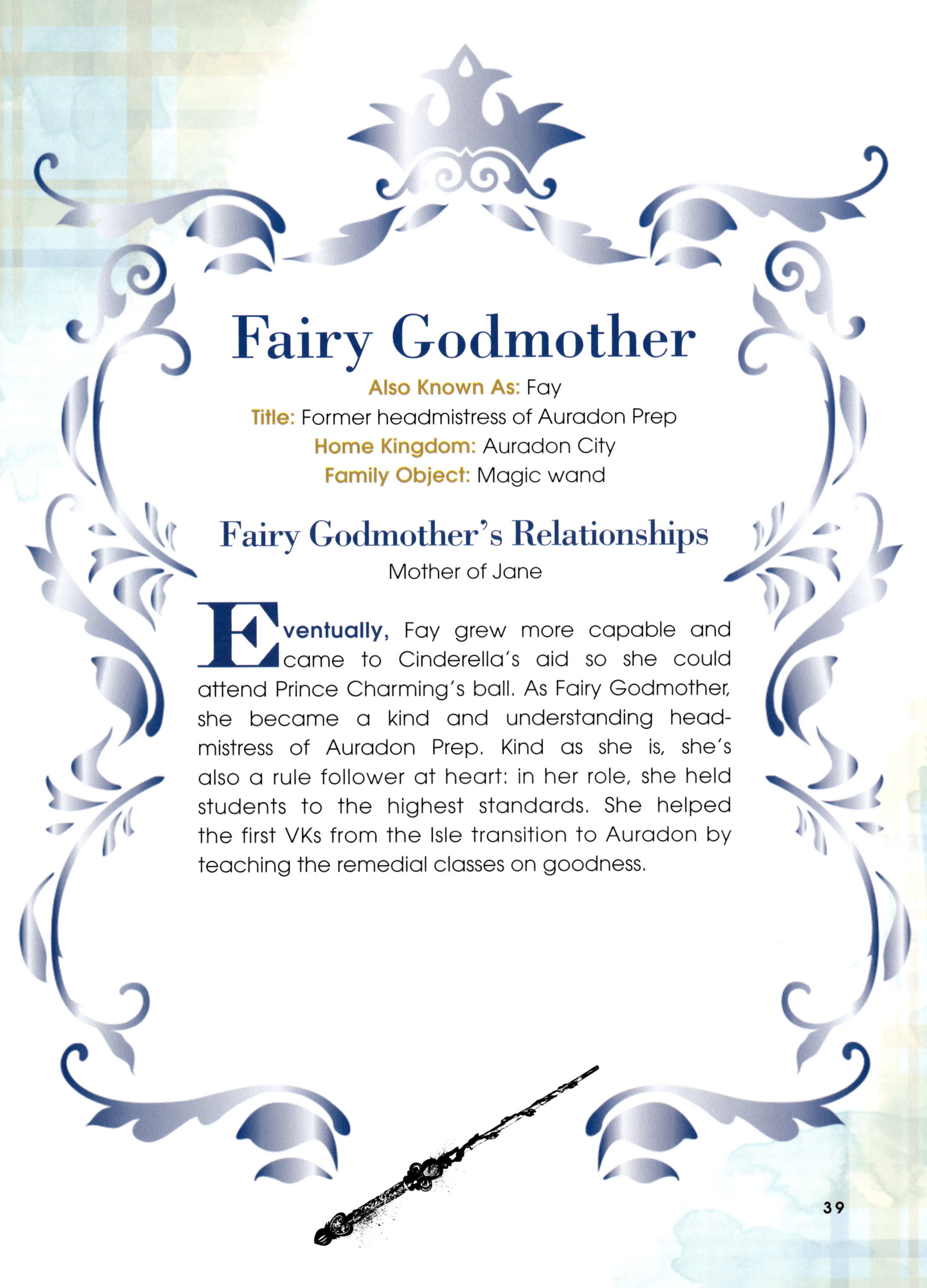

Fairy Godmother

Also Known As: Fay
Title: Former headmistress of Auradon Prep
Home Kingdom: Auradon City
Family Object: Magic wand

Fairy Godmother's Relationships

Mother of Jane

Eventually, Fay grew more capable and came to Cinderella's aid so she could attend Prince Charming's ball. As Fairy Godmother, she became a kind and understanding headmistress of Auradon Prep. Kind as she is, she's also a rule follower at heart: in her role, she held students to the highest standards. She helped the first VKs from the Isle transition to Auradon by teaching the remedial classes on goodness.

Aurora

Prince Phillip

Queen Leah

King Ben

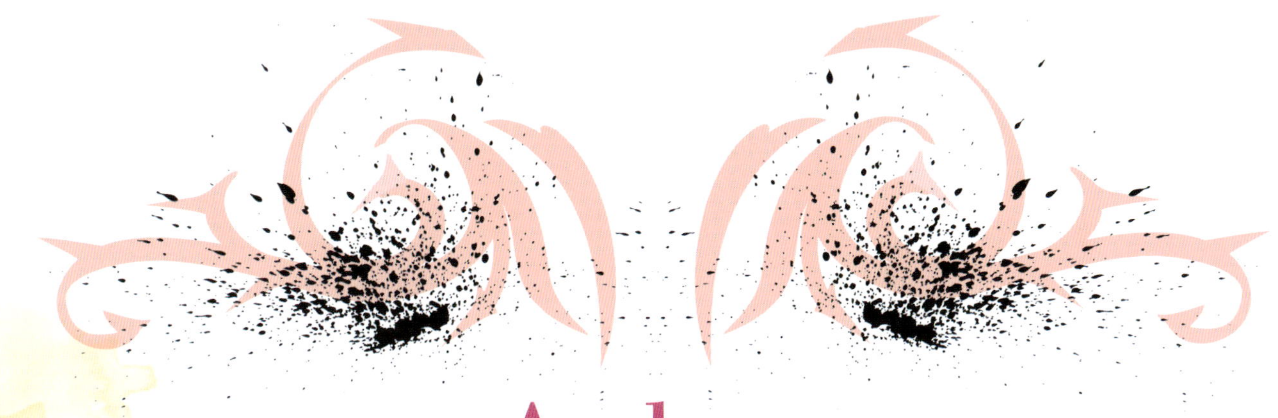

Audrey

Affiliation: Auradon Kid (AK)
Home Kingdom: Auroria

Audrey's Relationships

Daughter of Princess Aurora and Prince Phillip
Granddaughter of Queen Leah
Dated King Ben

Audrey can be peppy and vivacious, but she also has a jealous streak. She happily dated Ben before Mal came to Auradon, and she always believed she was destined to be the next queen of Auradon. After Ben and Mal started dating, she became angry—and her bitterness only grew when they got engaged. She broke into the Museum of Cultural History to steal the queen's crown and Maleficent's scepter in order to curse all of Auradon. Mal and Uma worked together to break her curses, and Hades used his ember to bring her back from the deathlike state that followed. After all they'd been through in the battle, Audrey apologized and made her peace with Mal and Ben. In fact, she even became their wedding planner!

Queen Leah

Title: Queen of Auroria
Home Kingdom: Auroria

Aurora

Audrey

Queen Leah's Relationships

Mother of Princess Aurora
Grandmother of Audrey

Queen Leah is a kind and caring ruler. However, she struggles with the sadness and bitterness of having lost time with Aurora as a child while Aurora was hidden away from Maleficent. Her suspicion toward villains extended to their children. When Mal came on the scene, Queen Leah did not believe that she was trustworthy. Queen Leah was in favor of keeping the magical barrier raised at the Isle of the Lost and did not want the VKs to come to Auradon. However, after watching the VKs save her granddaughter, she realized that her beliefs were wrong. Now she knows that Mal is not like her mother, and that she is a worthy queen of Auradon.

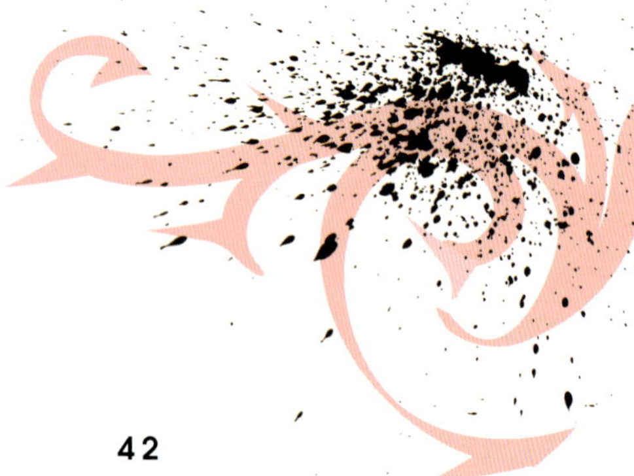

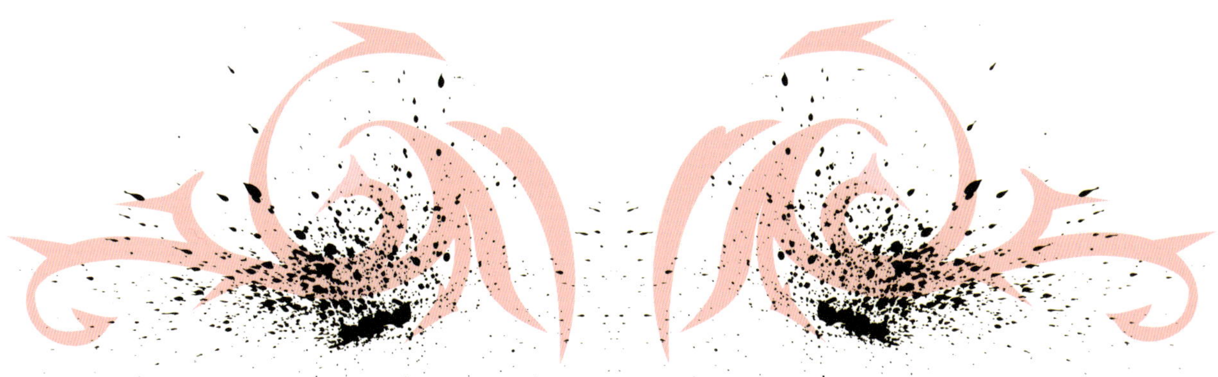

Aurora and Phillip

Titles: Princess and prince of Auroria
Home Kingdom: Auroria
Family Object: Aurora's spinning wheel

Queen Leah

Aurora and Phillip's Relationships

Daughter and son-in-law of Queen Leah
Parents of Audrey

Audrey

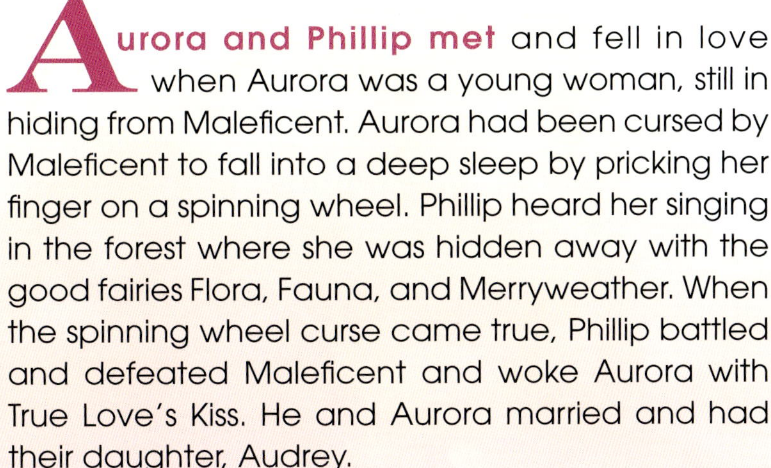

Aurora and Phillip met and fell in love when Aurora was a young woman, still in hiding from Maleficent. Aurora had been cursed by Maleficent to fall into a deep sleep by pricking her finger on a spinning wheel. Phillip heard her singing in the forest where she was hidden away with the good fairies Flora, Fauna, and Merryweather. When the spinning wheel curse came true, Phillip battled and defeated Maleficent and woke Aurora with True Love's Kiss. He and Aurora married and had their daughter, Audrey.

MOTTOES

In the world of Auradon, you've got to know exactly what you stand for. Some people can describe their core beliefs in one short sentence—even if they eventually change their minds, like Mal. Some of Auradon's most notable citizens have their own mottoes:

EVIE:
GOOD IS THE NEW BAD.

RED:
I'M A ONE-GIRL RIOT.

ELLA:
SOMETIMES YOU GOTTA GET YOUR HANDS DIRTY.

MAL:
ROTTEN TO THE CORE.

MALEFICENT:
POWER OVER ALL.

JAFAR:
THERE'S NO TEAM IN "I."

THE QUEEN OF HEARTS:
OFF WITH THEIR HEAD!

BRIDGET:
YOU GET MORE WITH SUGAR THAN SALT!

FAIRY GODMOTHER:
CHOOSE GOOD—ALWAYS.

AURADON PREP:
GOODNESS DOESN'T GET ANY BETTER.

ULIANA:
FIERCE, FEARED, AND THE BADDEST HERE.

Cinderella

King Charming

Chad

Chloe

Affiliation: Auradon Kid (AK)
Home Kingdom: Cinderellasburg
Family Object: Cinderella's glass slipper

Chloe's Relationships

Daughter of Cinderella and King Charming
Sister of Chad Charming

Chloe's childhood matched her family name: charming. She wanted for nothing growing up and prides herself on being a good rule-following person. Chloe is kind but can also be a bit naive: she doesn't always understand the difficulties others face. She's a talented sword fighter and has always wanted to compete on the swords and shields team at AuradonPrep. She loves both of her parents very much and wants to grow up to be just like her mother.

Chad

Affiliation: Auradon Kid (AK)
Home Kingdom: Cinderellasburg
Family Object: Cinderella's glass slipper

Chad's Relationships

Son of Cinderella and King Charming
Brother of Chloe Charming
Dated Audrey

At first glance, Chad is attractive, charming, and talented at athletics. At Auradon Prep, he played tourney with Jay and Carlos and was also on the swords and shields team. However, he has a tendency to be entitled and selfish. He wasn't open-minded toward the VKs, and he's known to use his good looks to get what he wants. He dated Audrey after Ben broke up with her, and he chose to side with her when she cursed Auradon. Mal and Evie agree: **he's the worst.**

Cinderella
King Charming
Chloe
Audrey

Ella

Also Known As: Cinderella
Home Kingdom: Cinderellasburg
Family Object: Glass slipper

Ella's Relationships

Stepsister of Drizella and Anastasia
Stepdaughter of Lady Tremaine

When Ella was young, she lived with Lady Tremaine and went to school at Merlin Academy. Her stepmother and stepsisters treated her horribly, and she was forced to cook and clean for them, acting as their servant. At school, Ella was very aware that she wasn't like many of her peers: she wasn't rich or royal, and she was mocked for coming to school wearing patched-up clothes. She did have one close friend, Bridget. However, she didn't trust most wealthy people and was especially put off by Prince Charming with his flirty (almost arrogant) demeanor.

When she is transported back in time by Maddox Hatter's pocketwatch, Chloe comes face to face with her mom, Ella, long before she has slid into her famous glass slippers.

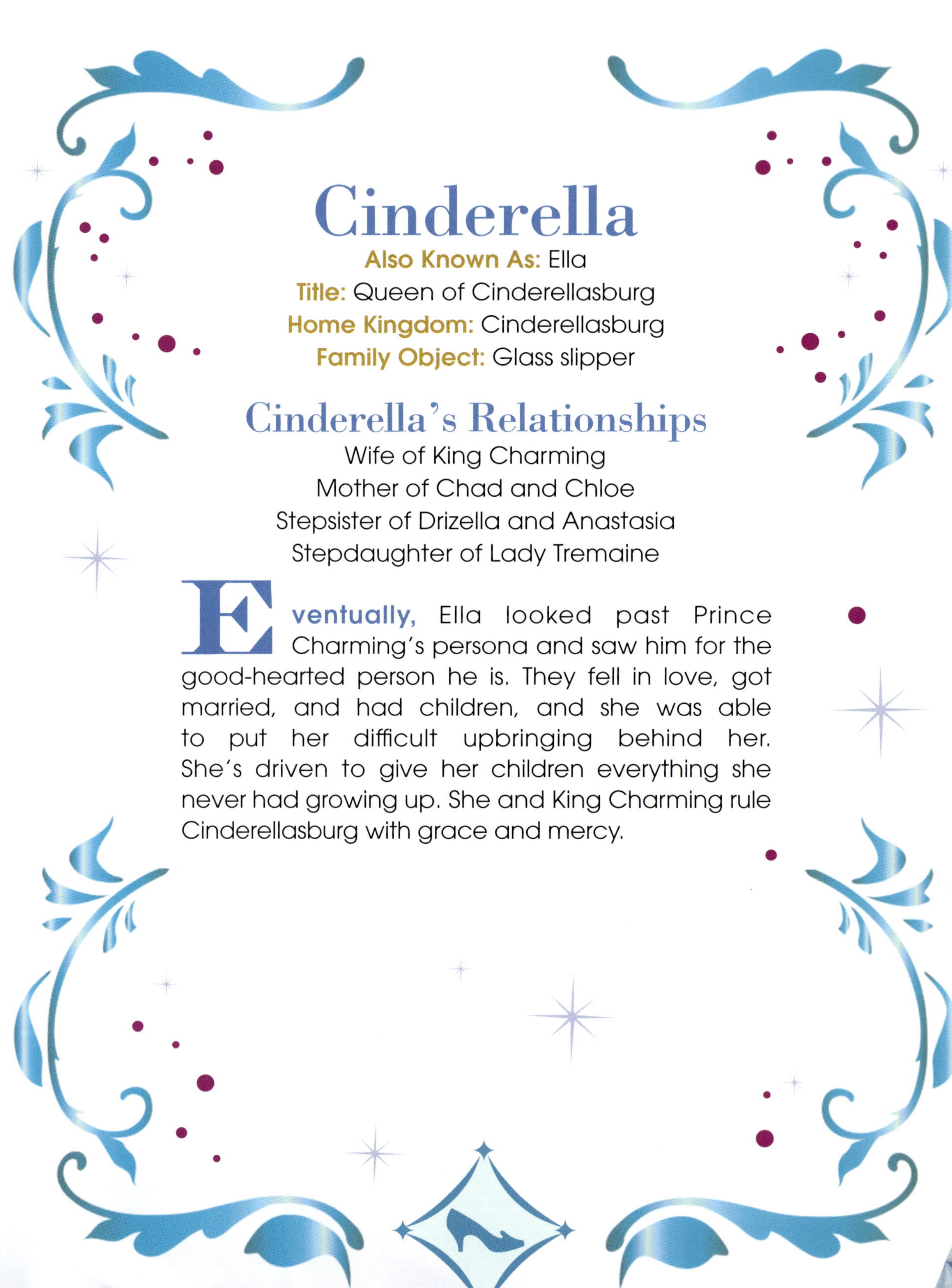

Cinderella

Also Known As: Ella
Title: Queen of Cinderellasburg
Home Kingdom: Cinderellasburg
Family Object: Glass slipper

Cinderella's Relationships

Wife of King Charming
Mother of Chad and Chloe
Stepsister of Drizella and Anastasia
Stepdaughter of Lady Tremaine

Eventually, Ella looked past Prince Charming's persona and saw him for the good-hearted person he is. They fell in love, got married, and had children, and she was able to put her difficult upbringing behind her. She's driven to give her children everything she never had growing up. She and King Charming rule Cinderellasburg with grace and mercy.

King Charming
Chad
Chloe
D
Drizella
A
Anastasia
Lady Tremaine

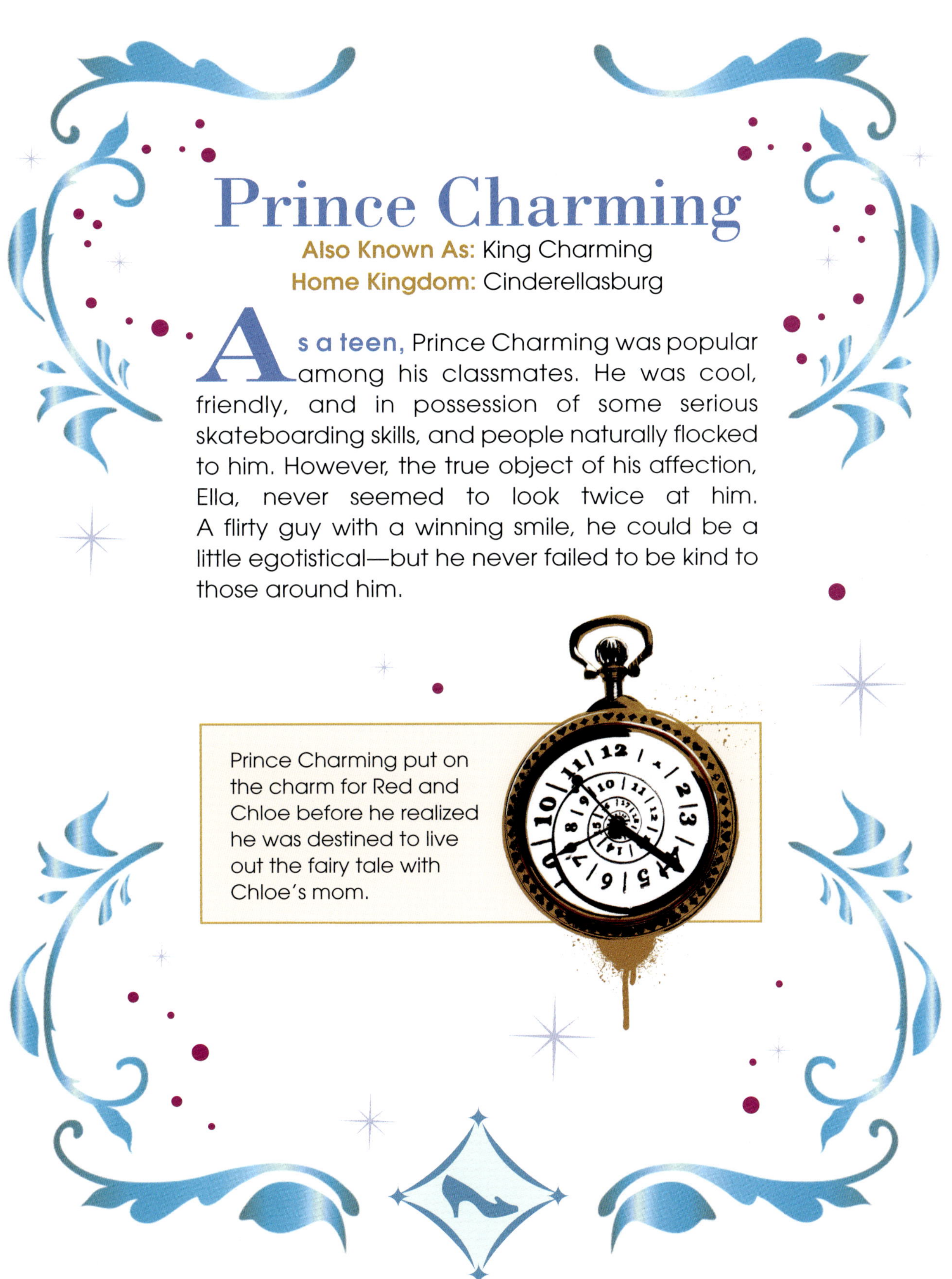

Prince Charming

Also Known As: King Charming
Home Kingdom: Cinderellasburg

As a teen, Prince Charming was popular among his classmates. He was cool, friendly, and in possession of some serious skateboarding skills, and people naturally flocked to him. However, the true object of his affection, Ella, never seemed to look twice at him. A flirty guy with a winning smile, he could be a little egotistical—but he never failed to be kind to those around him.

Prince Charming put on the charm for Red and Chloe before he realized he was destined to live out the fairy tale with Chloe's mom.

Cinderella

Chad

Chloe

King Charming

Also Known As: Prince Charming
Title: King of Cinderellasburg
Home Kingdom: Cinderellasburg

King Charming's Relationships

Husband of Cinderella
Father of Chad and Chloe

Prince Charming grew into a fair king in his own right and never stopped caring for Ella. As they grew older, he and Ella became close and eventually fell in love. Now he rules Cinderellasburg by Cinderella's side and loves to spend time with his two children—especially watching their athletic matches.

DECOR

A person's home can say a lot about their personality, and that's definitely true in the world of Auradon! The Queen of Hearts' palace shows off her love of red and her cold, hard-hearted personality, while Cinderella and King Charming's castle is filled with warm and cozy details. Evie has her own starter castle that's absolutely perfect for her. It gives her privacy in the forest, as well as lots of space for creating her latest fashion designs in her glass solarium.

The villains on the Isle of the Lost make sure their homes represent them, too, even if their living spaces are a bit less . . . wholesome. Hades lives in an underground lair, complete with lots of blue accents to match his hair and barking dogs to scare people away. Uliana's lair is even more over the top: it's made of a petrified sea creature! The creepy interior matches her personality, and even the furniture is made of bones. She hides her lair away in the Black Lagoon, with sea creatures to guard the entrance.

Top: Evie designs fashions in her sunny starter castle.
Below: Hades hides away in his underground home on the Isle of the Lost.

Lonnie

Affiliation: Auradon Kid (AK)
Home Kingdom: Northern Wei

Lonnie's Relationships

Daughter of Mulan and Li Shang

Lonnie is brave, strong, and kind. She's a leader and a loyal friend to both AKs and VKs. When Ben was captured by Uma, Lonnie was happy to join the group and head to the Isle of the Lost to bring him back home safely.

Though the sport of swords and shields had historically not allowed girls to compete, Lonnie was named captain of the team at Auradon Prep for her swordsmanship and leadership skills.

Mulan

Home Kingdom: Northern Wei

Mulan's Relationships

Wife of Li Shang
Mother of Lonnie

Like her own daughter, Mulan is a fearless fighter and a loyal friend and daughter. When her father was recruited as an old man to fight the Huns, Mulan pretended to be his son in order to serve in the army as his replacement. She ultimately saved all of China from its enemies, earning her the respect of the Emperor, along with the love of the man fighting beside her, Li Shang.

Jasmine

Aladdin

Home Kingdom: Agrabah
Family Object: Magic carpet

Aladdin's Relationships

Boyfriend of Jasmine

When he was young, Aladdin lived as a "street rat" in Agrabah, dreaming of wealth and a better life. While trying to retrieve a magic lamp from the Cave of Wonders, he met the Genie, who could grant him three wishes. Aladdin wished to be a prince to impress Jasmine, the princess of Agrabah—but she wasn't swayed by "Prince Ali." Ultimately, Aladdin realized he needed to be himself to win her heart.

Aladdin

Jasmine

Title: Princess of Agrabah

Home Kingdom: Agrabah

Jasmine's Relationships

Girlfriend of Aladdin

Jasmine grew up in a palace of riches but was unhappy when her father pushed her to marry for political strategy instead of love. She fought against this and sent away all the princes who came to woo her. When Aladdin arrived at her palace, pretending to be a prince, she wasn't interested in him, either. It wasn't until he finally showed her his real self that she fell in love with who he was inside. Now they are practically inseparable.

Dopey

Evie

Doug

Affiliation: Auradon Kid (AK)
Home Kingdom: Charmington

Doug's Relationships

Son of Dopey
Boyfriend of Evie

Doug can be a little shy at first, but he's also smart, open-minded, loyal, and kind. He has a fun sense of style—he loves wearing bow ties—and is a talented musician. He played in the Auradon Prep marching band but dreams of being in a rock band as an adult. When Evie first came to Auradon as a VK, Doug immediately welcomed her and helped her in her classes, even when other AKs were less sure. He loves Evie and is very supportive of her dreams, including her fashion design business.

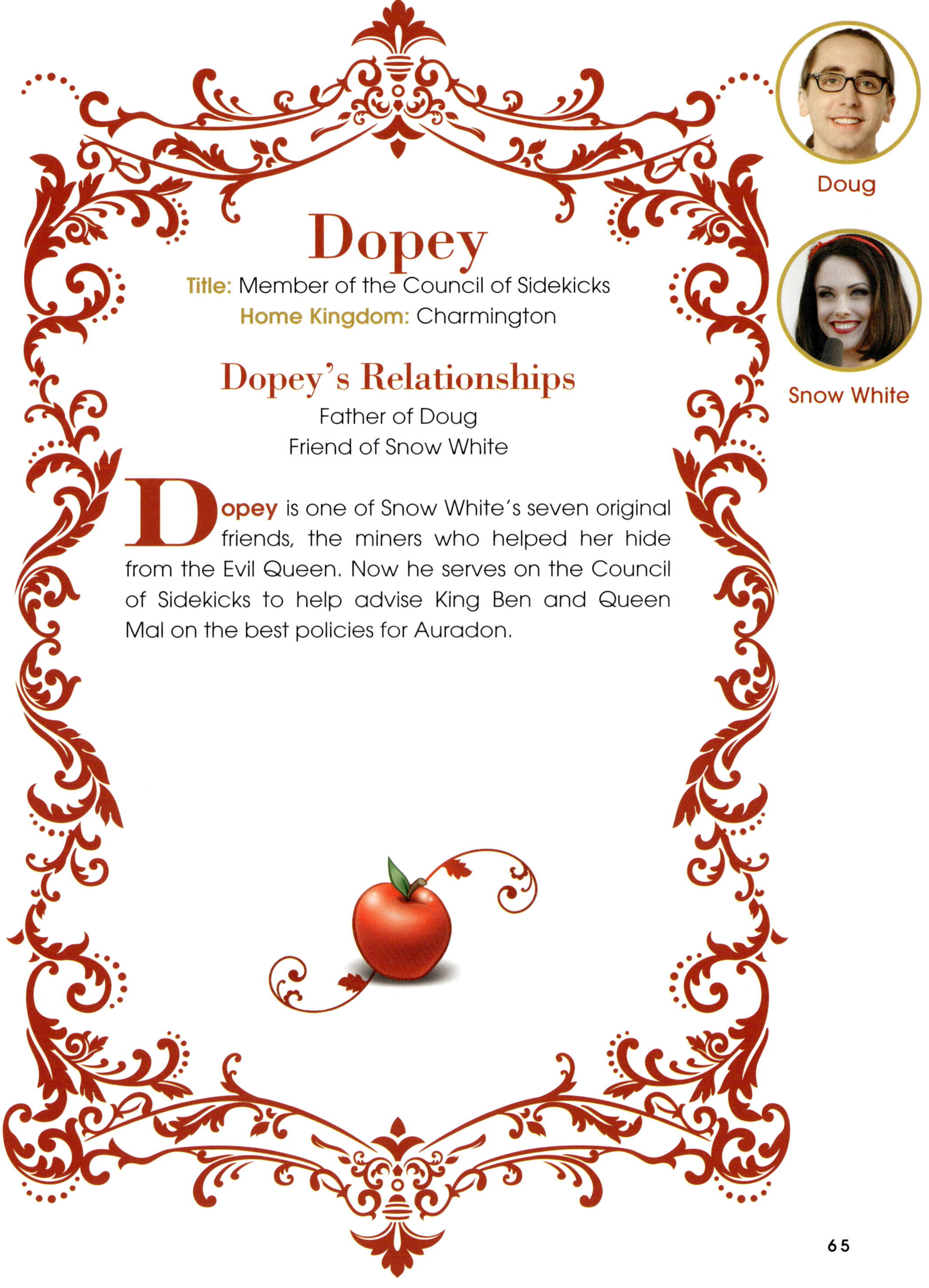

Dopey

Title: Member of the Council of Sidekicks

Home Kingdom: Charmington

Dopey's Relationships

Father of Doug

Friend of Snow White

Dopey is one of Snow White's seven original friends, the miners who helped her hide from the Evil Queen. Now he serves on the Council of Sidekicks to help advise King Ben and Queen Mal on the best policies for Auradon.

Doug

Snow White

Merlin

Title: Former headmaster of Merlin Academy

Home Kingdom: Camelot Heights

Merlin was an excellent headmaster and a great wizard who cared deeply about his students at Merlin Academy. An extremely powerful magic user, he could transform objects and people, and he could spell inanimate objects to do his bidding. In his old age, he often forgot where he'd placed things, and could be seen searching for items he had stashed in his sweeping robes—whether they were important scrolls or lit candles.

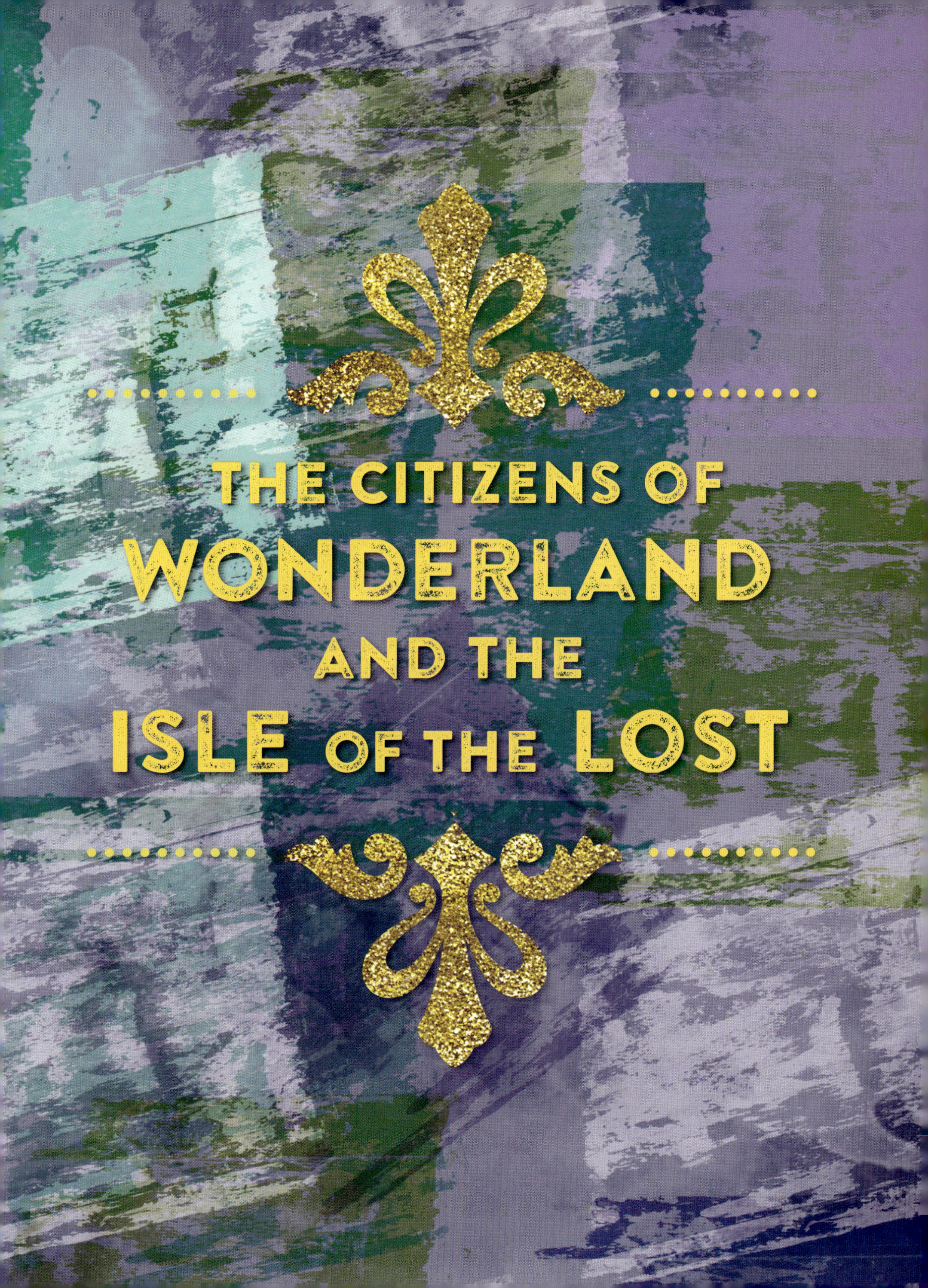
THE CITIZENS OF
WONDERLAND
AND THE
ISLE OF THE LOST

RED

Title: Princess of Wonderland
Affiliation: Villain Kid (VK)
Home Kingdom: Wonderland
Family Objects: Looking Glass, deck of playing cards

RED'S RELATIONSHIPS

Daughter of the Queen of Hearts

Red is bold and impulsive, a true rule breaker. She's spent her entire life being controlled by her mother's expectations. She's never been allowed to travel outside of Wonderland, and she desperately wishes to break free from her mom's restrictions. At the same time, she wants her mom's approval, though it's very difficult to come by. The Queen of Hearts will only be happy if Red rules at her side, and Red isn't interested in that future.

When Red has to go back in time to change the past and save her teenage mother from a vicious prank, she ends up stuck there with Chloe Charming. At first, she can't stand the rule-following princess, but Red's feelings change as she gets to know Chloe. Eventually, Red realizes she's stronger and better off when she has a trusted friend by her side.

The Queen of Hearts

BRIDGET

Also Known As: The Queen of Hearts
Home Kingdom: Wonderland
Family Objects: Looking Glass, deck of playing cards

As a teen, Bridget was the sweetest person in all of Merlin Academy. Her greatest wish was to make friends and be accepted by others at school. She loved to bake and to share all her magical treats, especially her hot-pink Fabulous Flamingo Feather Cupcakes, with the other students. She thought she could win over even the biggest of bullies with kindness and sugary baked goods.

After traveling back in time with the help of a magical pocketwatch, Red meets a fun-loving baker named Bridget, who happens to be a teenage version of her mom.

Red

THE QUEEN OF HEARTS

Also Known As: Bridget
Title: Queen of Wonderland
Home Kingdom: Wonderland
Family Objects: Looking Glass, deck of playing cards

THE QUEEN OF HEARTS' RELATIONSHIPS

Mother of Red

After a horrible prank, Bridget's heart grew cold, and she eventually grew into the Queen of Hearts. She decided that others could not be trusted and must be ruled with an iron fist. Now she's a tyrant—stubborn, inflexible, and without empathy.

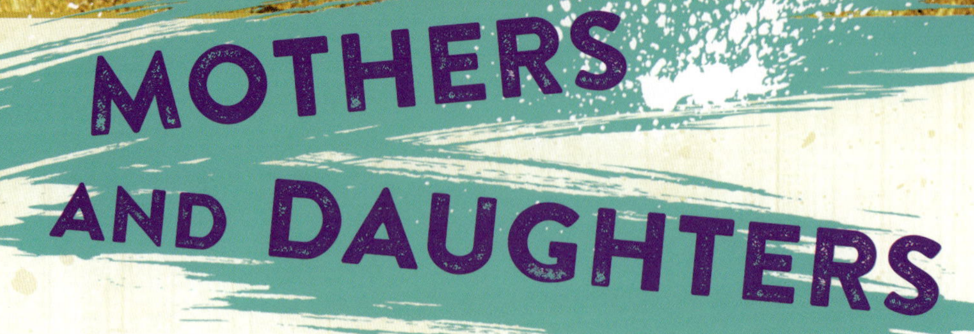

MOTHERS AND DAUGHTERS

Mother-daughter relationships can be complicated. Some daughters grow up idolizing their moms, and others don't want to be anything like them! It's just so in Auradon, the Isle of the Lost, and Wonderland.

Take Red and the Queen of Hearts: they couldn't be more different. The Queen of Hearts is set on ruling Wonderland with an iron fist—dictating what people eat, what they wear, and even what color the roses are. But Red is determined to have her own style, and to do something other than rule Wonderland at her mother's side. She wants a life that her mom can't control.

On the other hand, Chloe adores her mom, Cinderella. She sees her as the poised and perfect ruler of Cinderellasburg. Jane and Fairy Godmother, too, are close: they worked together to make Auradon Prep a wonderful and well-organized school.

Mal and Maleficent are an interesting pair, because their relationship changed over time. When she was young, Mal wanted nothing more than to make her mom proud by acting evil, just like her. She tried to mimic Maleficent's cruel and manipulative ways but ultimately decided she wasn't anything like her mom. Mal still loves her mother, but she is the true opposite of Maleficent: an open-minded, empathetic, kind ruler.

Top: Mal loves her mom, Maleficent, even if she doesn't always agree with her.
Below: Fairy Godmother and Jane both want what's best for the people of Auradon.

MADDOX HATTER

Title: Royal tutor
Home Kingdom: Wonderland

MADDOX HATTER'S RELATIONSHIPS

Son of the Mad Hatter

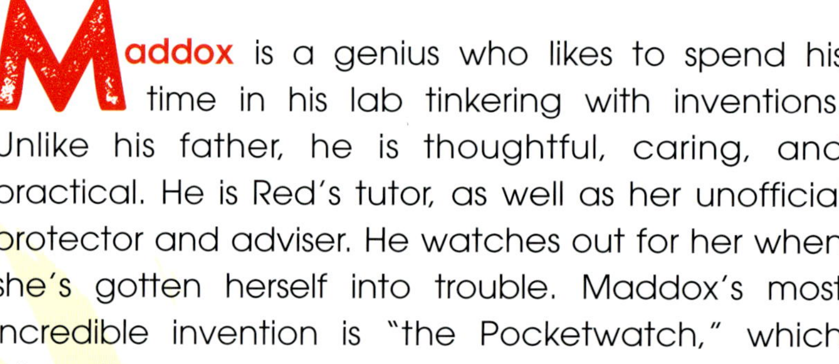

Maddox is a genius who likes to spend his time in his lab tinkering with inventions. Unlike his father, he is thoughtful, caring, and practical. He is Red's tutor, as well as her unofficial protector and adviser. He watches out for her when she's gotten herself into trouble. Maddox's most incredible invention is "the Pocketwatch," which allows the user to go back in time to the moment when they can get what their heart most desires.

The Mad Hatter

THE MAD HATTER

Home Kingdom: Wonderland

THE MAD HATTER'S RELATIONSHIPS

Father of Maddox

The Mad Hatter is known to be a very eccentric man who loves to throw over-the-top tea parties. He can be careless and frivolous, more caught up in spending time with friends or planning festivities than addressing important daily matters.

Maddox

MAL

Title: Queen of the United States of Auradon
Affiliation: Villain Kid (VK)
Home Kingdom: Isle of the Lost
Family Objects: Maleficent's spell book (which she donated to the Museum of Cultural History), Hades's ember

MAL'S RELATIONSHIPS

Daughter of Maleficent and Hades
Wife of Ben

Mal is a confident natural leader with street smarts. She was one of the first VKs invited to Auradon by Ben, the then prince. When she first arrived, she was set on stealing Fairy Godmother's wand to help her mother escape from the Isle of the Lost. But in time, she fell in love with both Ben and Auradon and decided she didn't need to follow in her mother's footsteps. There were times when she questioned whether she truly belonged in Auradon, particularly because she felt guilty about the VKs she'd left behind. Eventually, she helped convince the Auradon citizens to accept all VKs into Auradon Prep.

Mal is talented in lots of areas, both in artistic endeavors and in spells and magic. During her first months in Auradon, Mal often relied on her spell book to help her get by. She used spells to mess with other students, to convince Ben that he loved her, and to change herself in order to fit in as Ben's girlfriend. But once she realized she needed to ditch the spell book and learn to survive without magic, she was able to become the queen she was always meant to be.

Maleficent
Hades
Ben

Hades
Mal

MALEFICENT

Home Kingdom: Isle of the Lost
Family Objects: Spell book, scepter

MALEFICENT'S RELATIONSHIPS

Mother of Mal
Former wife of Hades
Frenemy of Evil Queen and ally of Jafar and Cruella De Vil

As a teen, Maleficent attended Merlin Academy. She dated Hades and hung out with Uliana, Morgie, and Hook. Even back then she was a bully, and she went on to become a vengeful and cruel villain as she grew older. She was exiled to the Isle of the Lost by King Beast and spent years planning her escape—and her revenge. When her daughter, Mal, was allowed to attend Auradon Prep, Maleficent tried to persuade her to steal Fairy Godmother's wand and release her from the Isle. However, Mal chose good and fought against her mother. Ultimately, after the battle at Ben's coronation, Maleficent turned into a lizard—reduced to a creature whose size matched the amount of love in her heart.

Maleficent
Mal

HADES

Title: Former lord of the Underworld
Home Kingdom: Isle of the Lost
Family Object: Magical ember

HADES'S RELATIONSHIPS

Father of Mal
Former husband of Maleficent

Teenage Hades attended Merlin Academy and spent his free time with some of the other villains at the school, including Uliana, Hook, Morgie, and Maleficent. It was there that he and Maleficent started dating. Hades was sent to live on the Isle of the Lost by King Beast as an adult. He did not have a close relationship with Mal during her childhood, but he ultimately ended up helping her when she needed his ember to save Audrey. After that, they were closer than they'd been before, and Hades attended Mal's wedding to Ben.

TRANSFORMATIVE ABILITIES

The people of Auradon can surprise you in many ways—but one of the biggest shocks to newcomers is that some people can *transform*!

Mal inherited the ability to transform into a dragon from her mother, Maleficent. While she doesn't do this often, she will transform in times of danger, like when she had to stop her mom from ruining Ben's coronation ceremony or when she had to battle Uma. Like Mal, Uma is also able to transform: using Ursula's magic necklace, she can become a giant octopus.

Maleficent

Uma
Mal

CARLOS

Affiliation: Villain Kid (VK)
Home Kingdom: Isle of the Lost

CARLOS'S RELATIONSHIPS

Son of Cruella De Vil
Dated Jane

Carlos was an intelligent, witty, and caring person—a true and loyal friend to everyone. He was skilled with technology and even mastered dog speak. He never let fear stop him from being open-minded.

His mother had taught him to fear dogs, but after meeting Dude, he realized that dogs could make wonderful companions. He was a part of some of the biggest events in Auradon history and helped Mal, Evie, and Jay on countless occasions.

Cruella De Vil

Jane

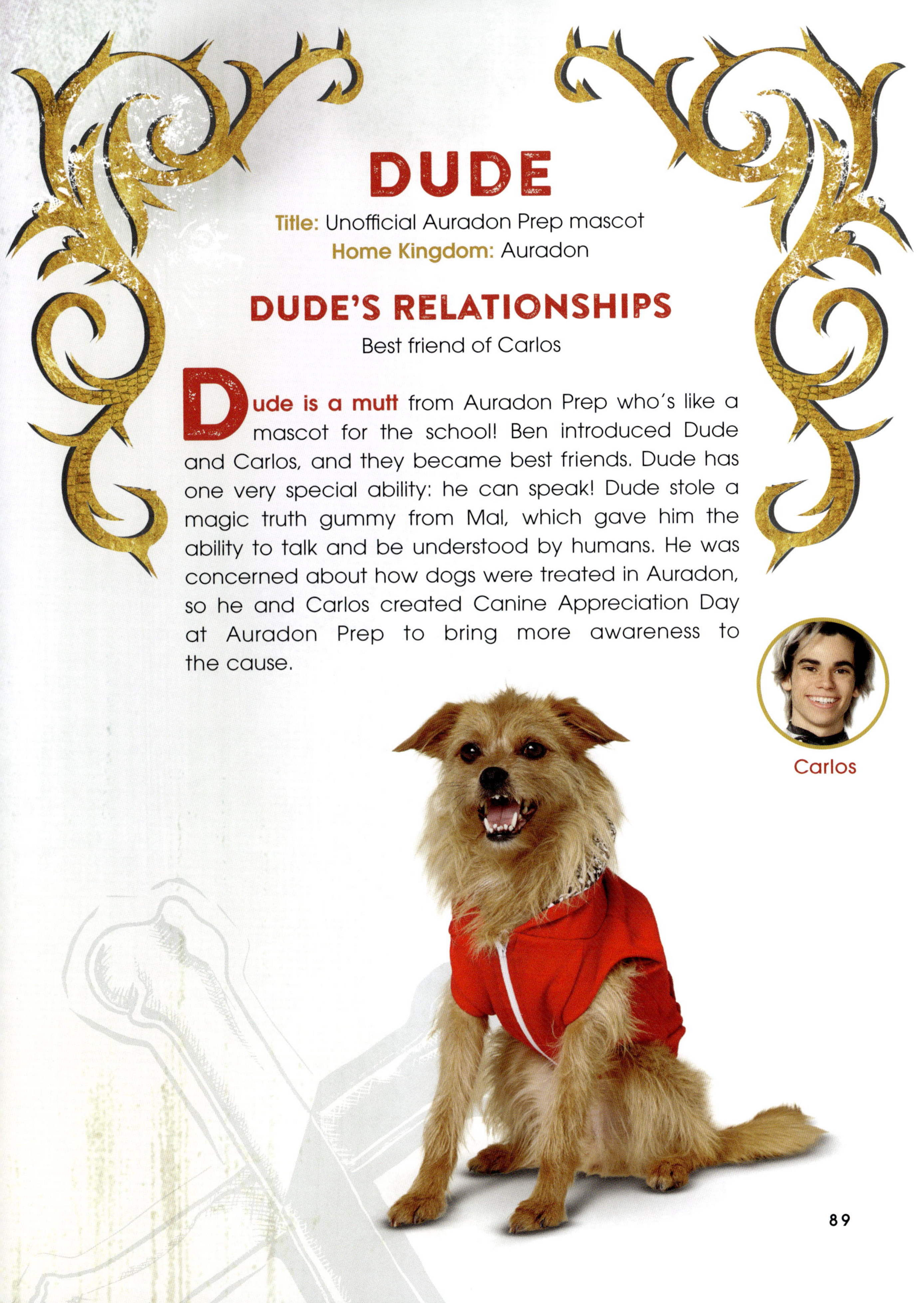

DUDE

Title: Unofficial Auradon Prep mascot
Home Kingdom: Auradon

DUDE'S RELATIONSHIPS

Best friend of Carlos

Dude is a mutt from Auradon Prep who's like a mascot for the school! Ben introduced Dude and Carlos, and they became best friends. Dude has one very special ability: he can speak! Dude stole a magic truth gummy from Mal, which gave him the ability to talk and be understood by humans. He was concerned about how dogs were treated in Auradon, so he and Carlos created Canine Appreciation Day at Auradon Prep to bring more awareness to the cause.

Carlos

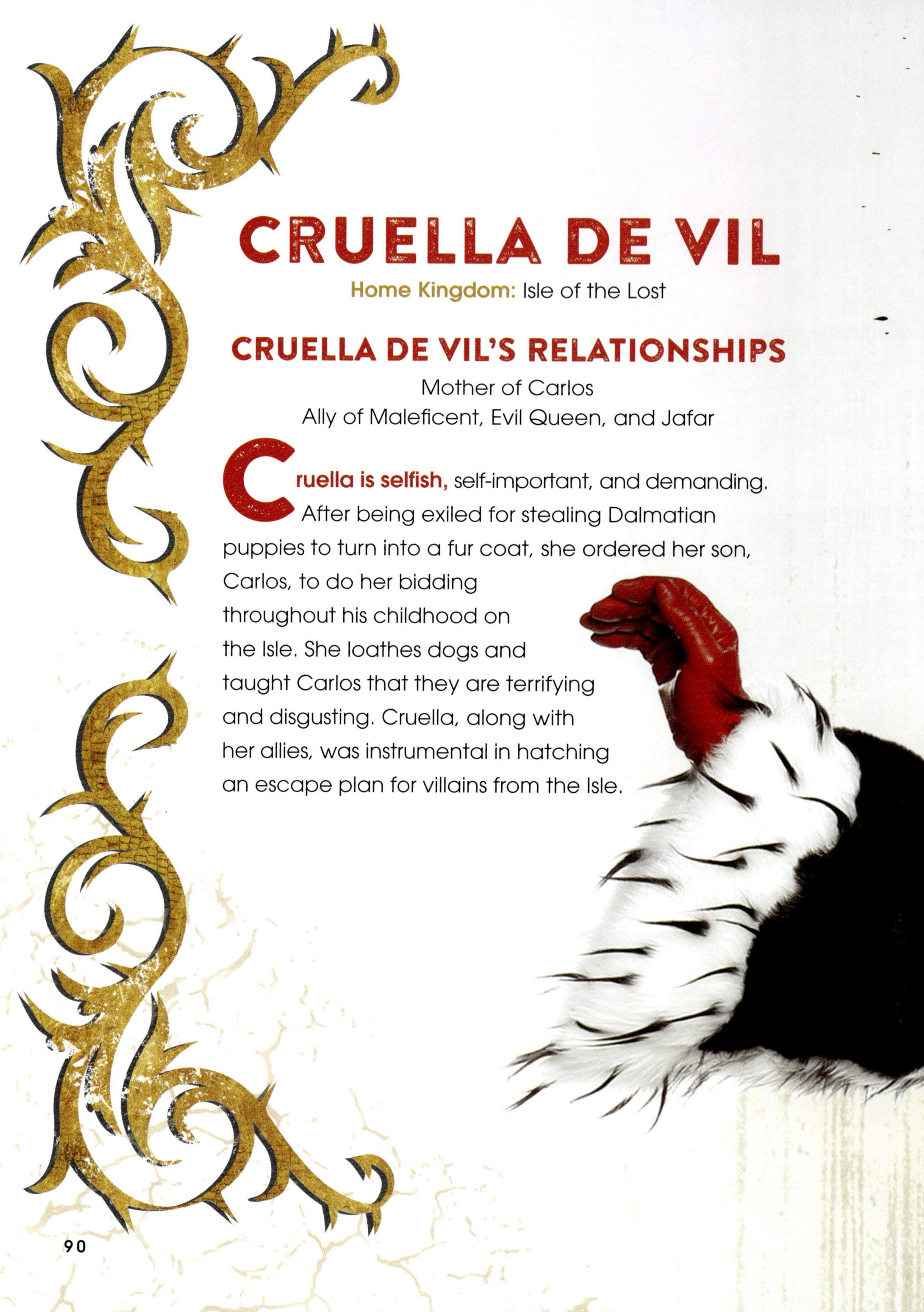

CRUELLA DE VIL

Home Kingdom: Isle of the Lost

CRUELLA DE VIL'S RELATIONSHIPS

Mother of Carlos
Ally of Maleficent, Evil Queen, and Jafar

Cruella is selfish, self-important, and demanding. After being exiled for stealing Dalmatian puppies to turn into a fur coat, she ordered her son, Carlos, to do her bidding throughout his childhood on the Isle. She loathes dogs and taught Carlos that they are terrifying and disgusting. Cruella, along with her allies, was instrumental in hatching an escape plan for villains from the Isle.

Carlos

EVIE

Affiliation: Villain Kid (VK)
Home Kingdom: Isle of the Lost
Family Object: Magic mirror (shard of mirror)

EVIE'S RELATIONSHIPS

Daughter of Evil Queen
Best friends with Mal
Girlfriend of Doug

Evie is charming and flirty, creative and artistic. When she first arrived in Auradon, she felt like her only value came from being beautiful and dating royalty—but she soon learned that she is much more than her appearance. Evie has incredible fashion sense and is now a respected designer in Auradon with her own business, Evie's 4 Hearts. She's very intelligent and particularly talented at chemistry and potions. Most important, she has a good heart and believes in finding the best in others. She fought alongside Mal, Jay, Carlos, and Ben to free the other VKs from the Isle of the Lost.

Evil Queen

Doug

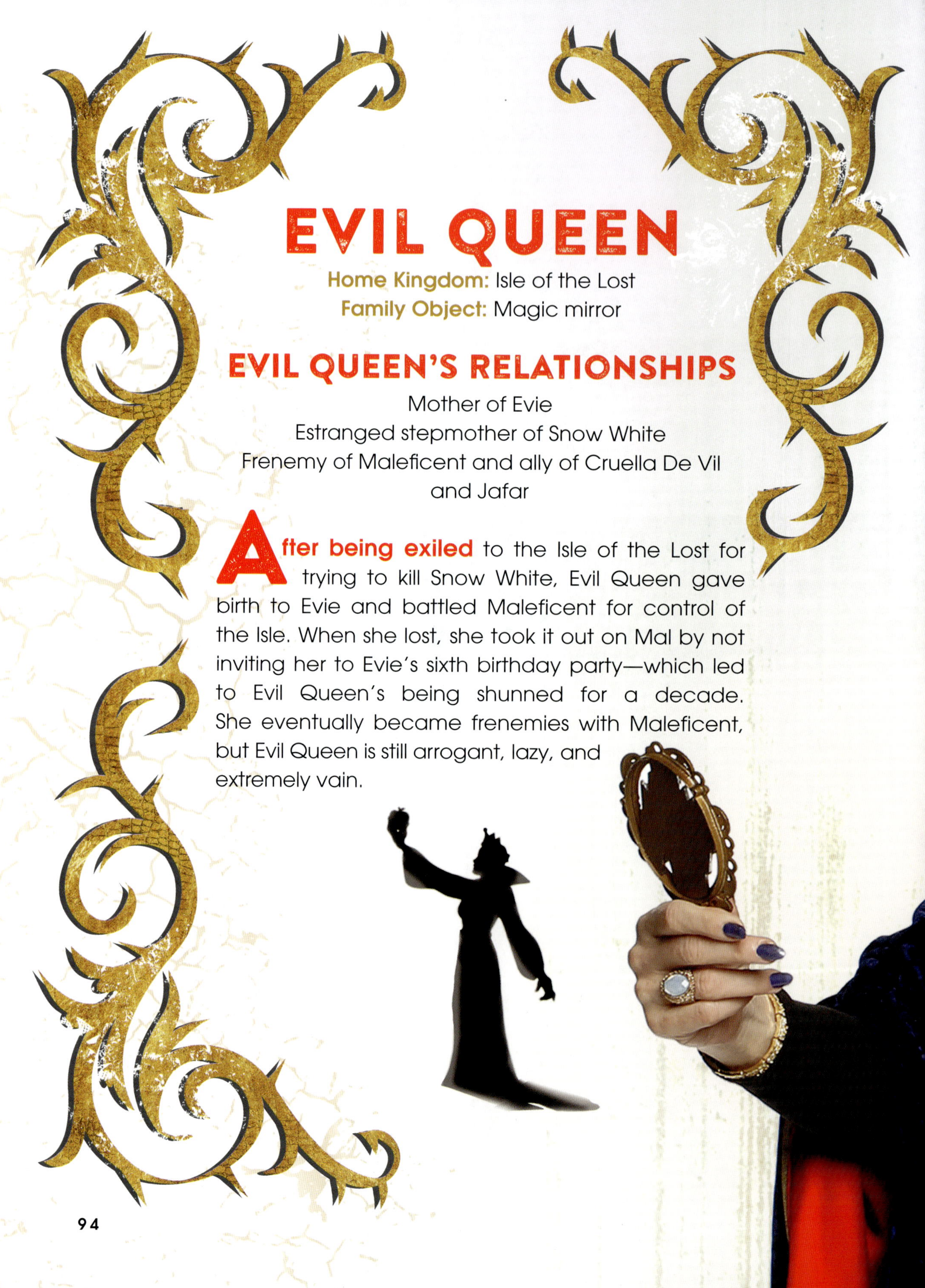

EVIL QUEEN

Home Kingdom: Isle of the Lost
Family Object: Magic mirror

EVIL QUEEN'S RELATIONSHIPS

Mother of Evie
Estranged stepmother of Snow White
Frenemy of Maleficent and ally of Cruella De Vil and Jafar

After being exiled to the Isle of the Lost for trying to kill Snow White, Evil Queen gave birth to Evie and battled Maleficent for control of the Isle. When she lost, she took it out on Mal by not inviting her to Evie's sixth birthday party—which led to Evil Queen's being shunned for a decade. She eventually became frenemies with Maleficent, but Evil Queen is still arrogant, lazy, and extremely vain.

Evie

PERSONAL
STYLE

Jafar

JAY

Affiliation: Villain Kid (VK)
Home Kingdom: Isle of the Lost

JAY'S FAMILY

Son of Jafar

Jay is athletic, fun, and loyal. He's very talented in sword fighting, parkour, and tourney. When he first came to Auradon, he looked out for himself only—but as time went on, he learned how to be a good team player. Since then, he's encouraged Carlos, Lonnie, and others to believe in themselves and their talents. He's always been supportive of the other VKs and will put himself in danger time and again to make sure the others are safe. After finishing school, he decided to travel so that he could see more of Auradon.

JAFAR

Home Kingdom: Isle of the Lost

JAFAR'S RELATIONSHIPS

Father of Jay
Ally of Maleficent, Evil Queen,
and Cruella De Vil

Jafar is a greedy schemer and a crooked diplomat. He was cast out of Agrabah and sent to the Isle of the Lost after trying to oust the Sultan and take over his kingdom. Since then, he has opened his own business, called Jafar's Junk Shop, which resells stolen items. He taught Jay to be a thief, just to boost profits for the store.

Jay

UMA

Title: Principal of Auradon Prep
Affiliation: Villain Kid (VK)
Home Kingdom: Isle of the Lost
Family Object: Ursula's magical shell necklace

UMA'S RELATIONSHIPS

Daughter of Ursula
Niece of Uliana

Uma is a confident and resourceful VK with a major mean streak. She spent many years working for her mother on the Isle of the Lost as a server for Ursula's Fish & Chips while also running the streets with her band of pirate rogues. When Mal was chosen to attend Auradon Prep, Uma was overwhelmed with envy. She wanted to bring down the magical barrier so she could escape the Isle while also getting revenge on Mal. She got her opportunity when Mal returned to the Isle: Uma and her allies captured Ben, who had come to convince Mal to return to Auradon. When Mal and her friends successfully freed Ben, Uma took it one step further by putting Ben under a magic love spell. She almost succeeded in bringing down the barrier during the Royal Cotillion, but Mal stopped her once again. Ultimately, Uma and Mal became reluctant allies when they needed to work together to stop Audrey from cursing all of Auradon. Their friendship helped push Mal to finally bring down the barrier between Auradon and the Isle. Since that time, Uma has successfully transitioned to life in Auradon. In fact, her transformation went so well that when Fairy Godmother retired as headmistress of Auradon Prep, Uma was promoted to the position.

Ursula

Uliana

Ursula

Uma

ULIANA

Home Kingdom: Isle of the Lost

ULIANA'S RELATIONSHIPS

Sister of Ursula
Aunt of Uma

Uliana was a sea witch and was the leader of the villains at Merlin Academy. She was a known bully and especially liked to torment Bridget and Ella. She wanted to be the biggest and baddest villain Merlin Academy had ever seen, and she'd take revenge on anyone who put her reputation in question. She was very competitive with her big sister, Ursula, who had created quite an evil reputation for herself during her time at Merlin Academy.

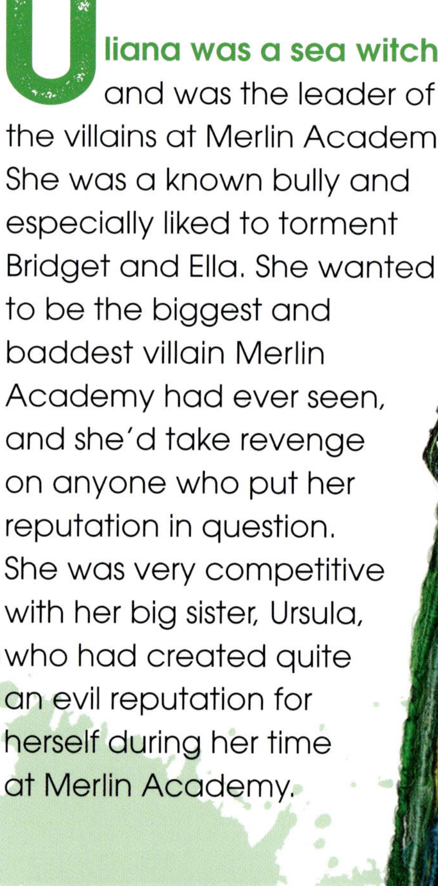

Uma

URSULA

Home Kingdom: Isle of the Lost
Family Objects: Magical shell necklace

Uliana

URSULA'S RELATIONSHIPS

Mother of Uma
Sister of Uliana

Ursula attended Merlin Academy, where she got plenty of practice bullying the other students and starting trouble. After being sent to live on the Isle of the Lost—thanks to some nasty business with Ariel—Ursula opened her restaurant, Ursula's Fish & Chips, and had her daughter, Uma.

D
Drizella
Cinderella
Lady
Tremaine

DIZZY

Affiliation: Villain Kid (VK)
Home Kingdom: Isle of the Lost

DIZZY'S RELATIONSHIPS

Daughter of Drizella, Cinderella's evil stepsister
Granddaughter of Lady Tremaine

Fun, energetic, and creative, Dizzy worked at her grandmother's salon, Curl Up & Dye, while she lived on the Isle of the Lost. However, she dreamed of going to Auradon, like Evie, whom she looks up to as a big sister. Also like Evie, Dizzy loves fashion and is a talented designer. Dizzy was chosen to be part of the second group of VKs to come to Auradon Prep—something that thrilled her.

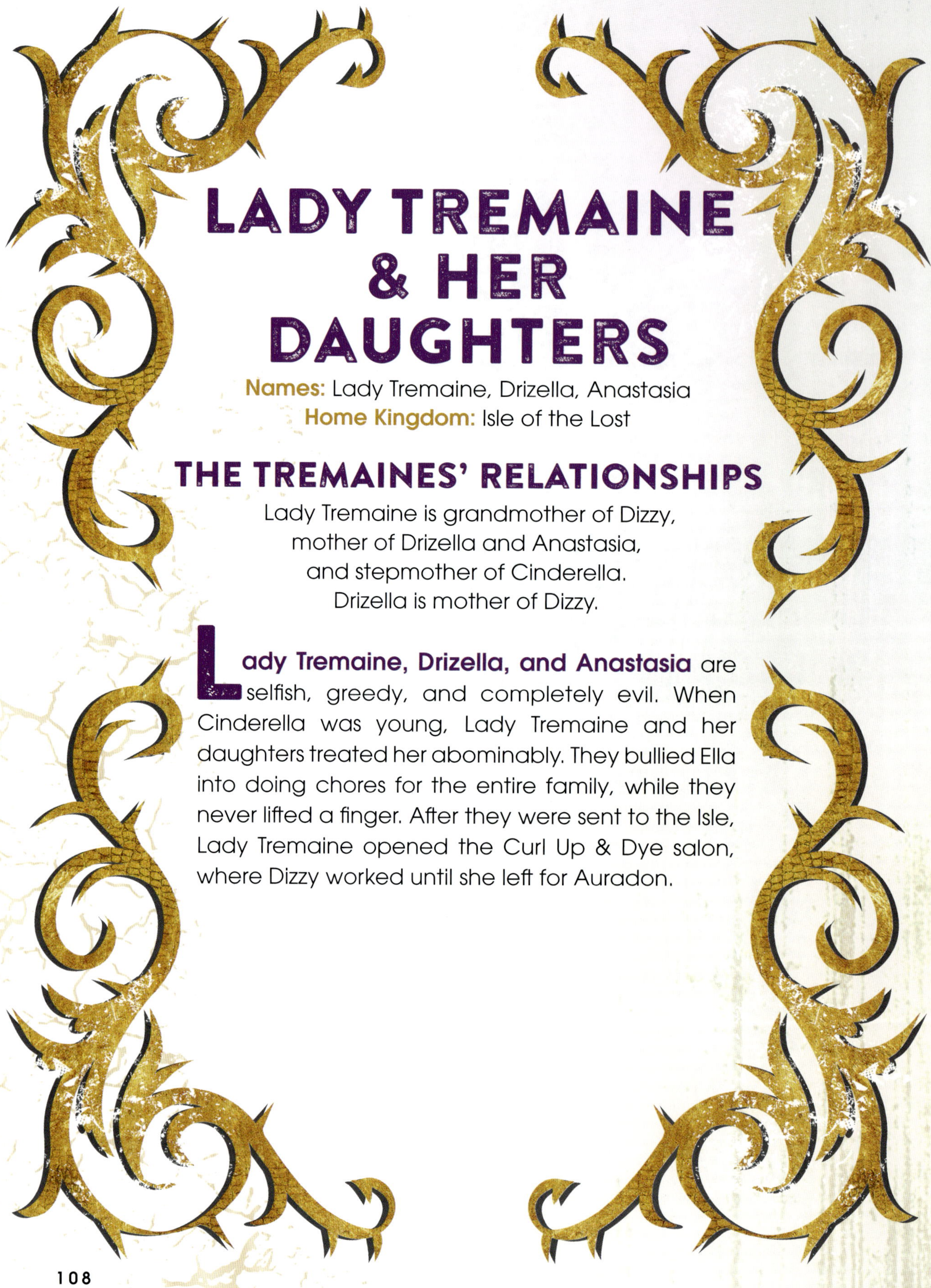

LADY TREMAINE & HER DAUGHTERS

Names: Lady Tremaine, Drizella, Anastasia
Home Kingdom: Isle of the Lost

THE TREMAINES' RELATIONSHIPS

Lady Tremaine is grandmother of Dizzy,
mother of Drizella and Anastasia,
and stepmother of Cinderella.
Drizella is mother of Dizzy.

Lady Tremaine, Drizella, and Anastasia are selfish, greedy, and completely evil. When Cinderella was young, Lady Tremaine and her daughters treated her abominably. They bullied Ella into doing chores for the entire family, while they never lifted a finger. After they were sent to the Isle, Lady Tremaine opened the Curl Up & Dye salon, where Dizzy worked until she left for Auradon.

Dizzy
D
Drizella
A
Anastasia
Cinderella

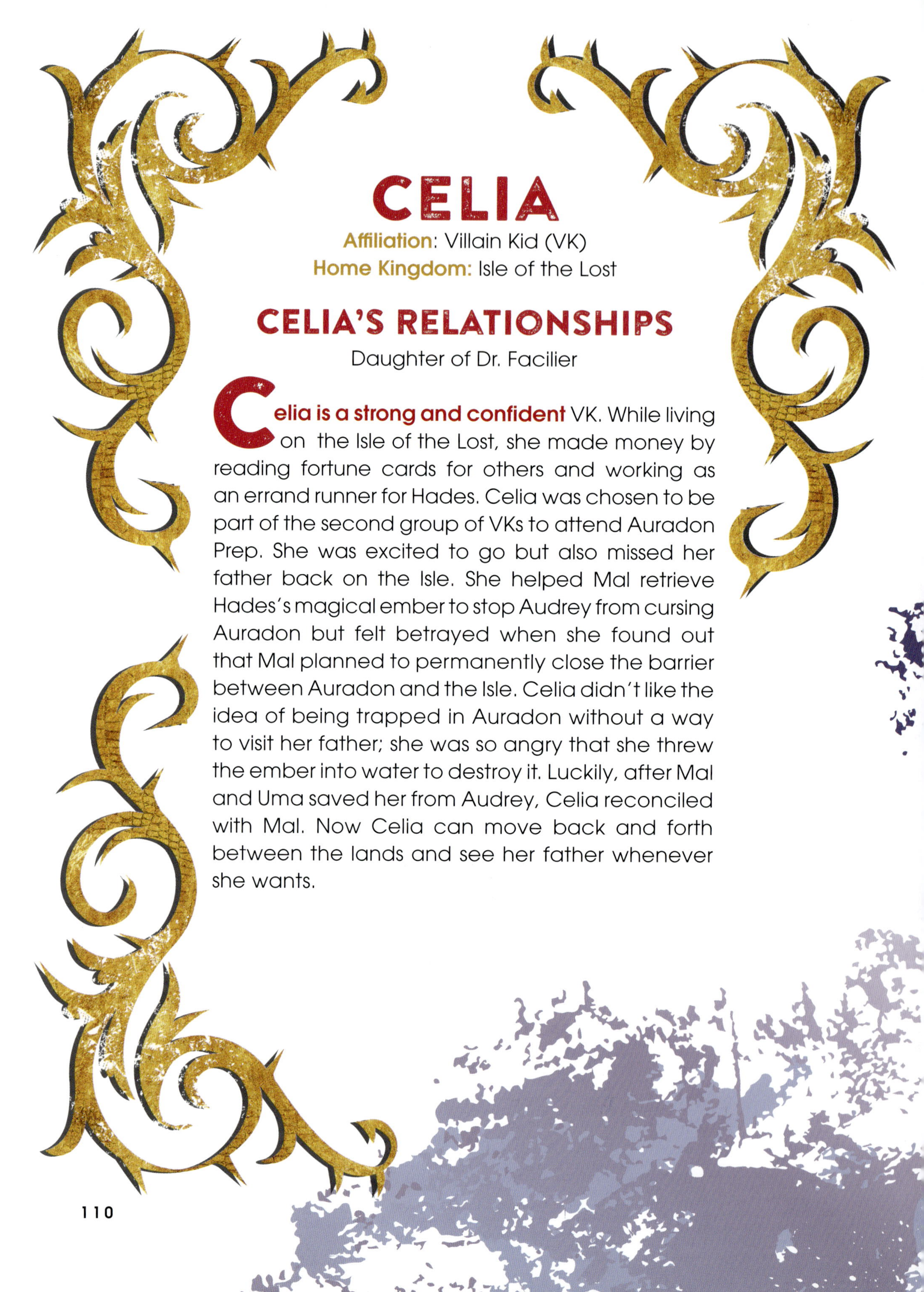

CELIA

Affiliation: Villain Kid (VK)
Home Kingdom: Isle of the Lost

CELIA'S RELATIONSHIPS

Daughter of Dr. Facilier

Celia is a strong and confident VK. While living on the Isle of the Lost, she made money by reading fortune cards for others and working as an errand runner for Hades. Celia was chosen to be part of the second group of VKs to attend Auradon Prep. She was excited to go but also missed her father back on the Isle. She helped Mal retrieve Hades's magical ember to stop Audrey from cursing Auradon but felt betrayed when she found out that Mal planned to permanently close the barrier between Auradon and the Isle. Celia didn't like the idea of being trapped in Auradon without a way to visit her father; she was so angry that she threw the ember into water to destroy it. Luckily, after Mal and Uma saved her from Audrey, Celia reconciled with Mal. Now Celia can move back and forth between the lands and see her father whenever she wants.

Dr. Facilier

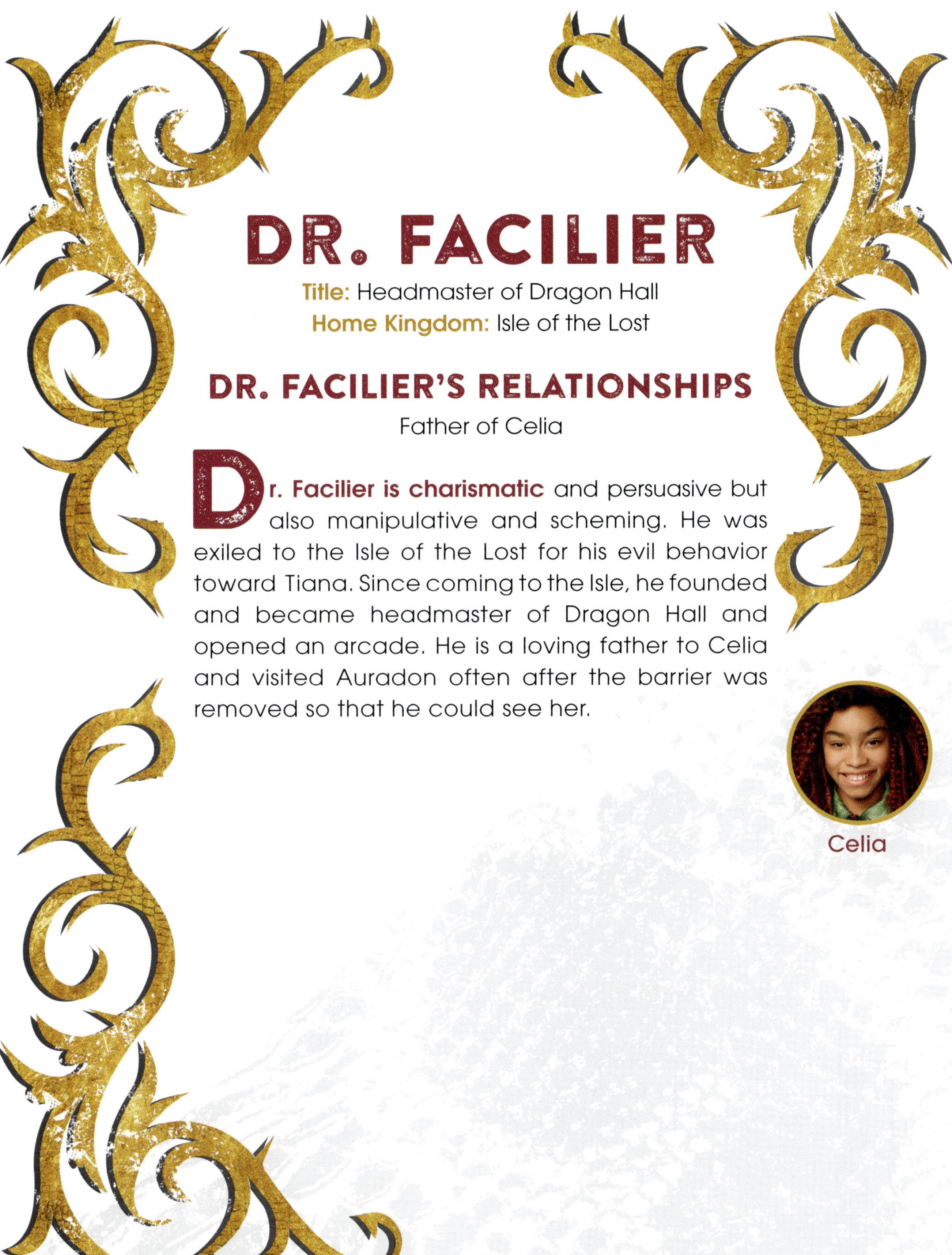

DR. FACILIER

Title: Headmaster of Dragon Hall
Home Kingdom: Isle of the Lost

DR. FACILIER'S RELATIONSHIPS

Father of Celia

Dr. Facilier is charismatic and persuasive but also manipulative and scheming. He was exiled to the Isle of the Lost for his evil behavior toward Tiana. Since coming to the Isle, he founded and became headmaster of Dragon Hall and opened an arcade. He is a loving father to Celia and visited Auradon often after the barrier was removed so that he could see her.

Celia

FAMILY BUSINESSES

For those who run a store, a school, or even a kingdom, what are the family dynamics like?

All across Auradon and the surrounding lands, families run shops, schools, and even kingdoms—whether they always get along or not.

Beast and Belle were incredibly supportive of Ben as he inherited the kingdom and learned to be a caring leader of Auradon. Now, as king and queen, Ben and Mal happily work together to make Auradon a safe and welcoming land. Similarly, Fairy Godmother spent many years overseeing Auradon Prep and relied on Jane to organize the best extracurriculars around. And it's not just Auradon families that are better together: Dr. Facilier's work as arcade owner and headmaster of Dragon Hall didn't get in the way of his love for his daughter, Celia.

But every family has their moments of bickering and resentment, particularly if they once lived on the Isle of the Lost. VKs haven't always loved working with their relatives. Uma worked at her mom's restaurant—Ursula's Fish & Chips—but always wished to get off the island and experience more than serving unruly customers. Dizzy worked at Curl Up & Dye, her grandmother's salon, but dreamed

of being a designer, like Evie. And Jay was happy to attend Auradon Prep and stop stealing for his father's junk shop.

Nevertheless, both AKs and VKs can learn valuable skills—and *sometimes* have fun—spending time with their families.

Left page: Uma was a waitress at her mom's seafood restaurant on the Isle of the Lost.

Above and Left: Dizzy ran her grandmother's salon on the Isle of the Lost.

Right: Jay was ready for a new adventure after spending years working at his dad's junk shop.

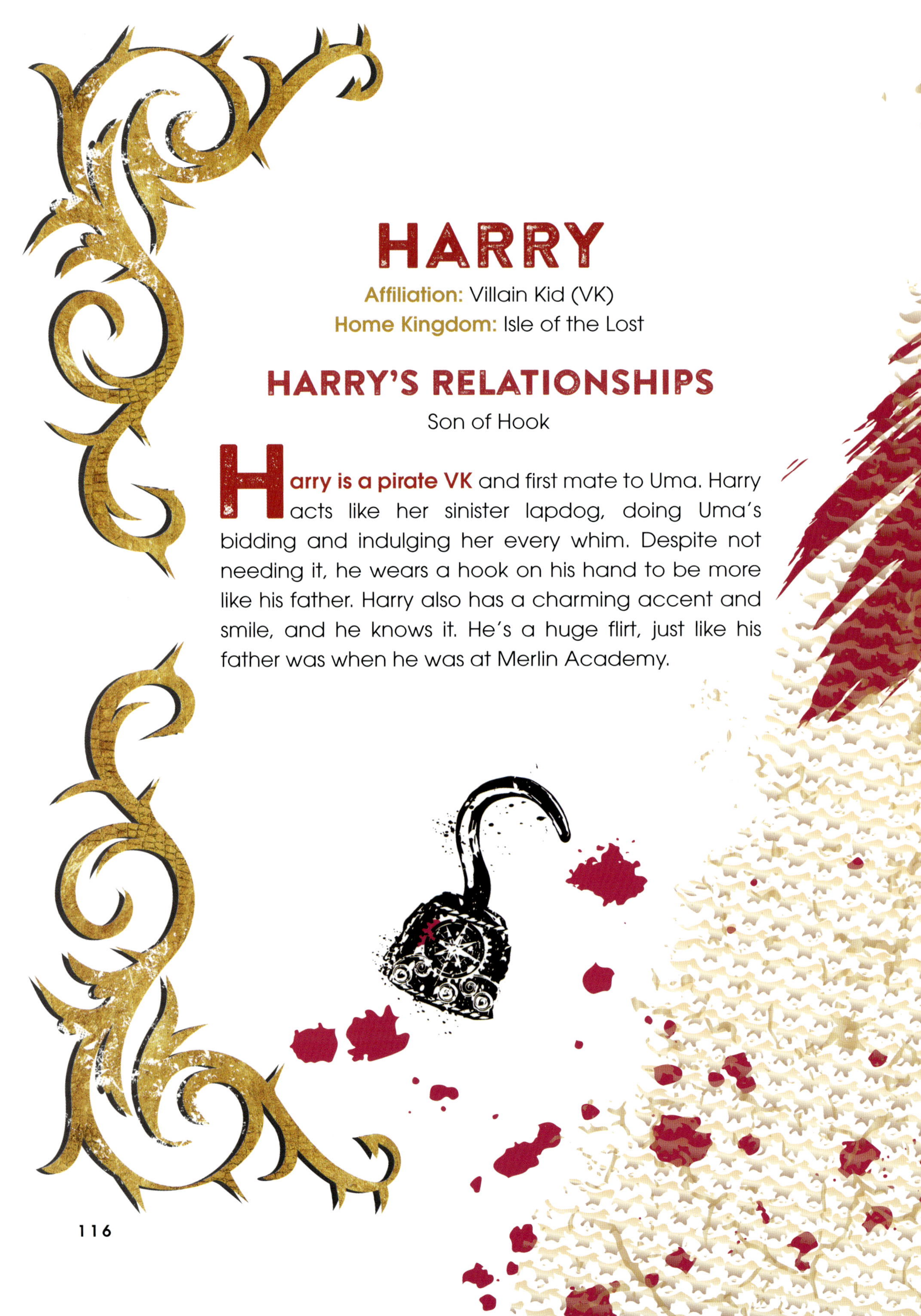

HARRY

Affiliation: Villain Kid (VK)
Home Kingdom: Isle of the Lost

HARRY'S RELATIONSHIPS

Son of Hook

Harry is a pirate VK and first mate to Uma. Harry acts like her sinister lapdog, doing Uma's bidding and indulging her every whim. Despite not needing it, he wears a hook on his hand to be more like his father. Harry also has a charming accent and smile, and he knows it. He's a huge flirt, just like his father was when he was at Merlin Academy.

Hook

Harry

HOOK

Home Kingdom: Isle of the Lost

HOOK'S RELATIONSHIPS

Father of Harry

Hook was exiled to the Isle of the Lost for battling Peter Pan. As a teen, Hook hung out in a clique with Uliana, Morgie, Maleficent, and Hades. He loved being mean to the other students. His favorite move was threatening to make them walk the plank. He is arrogant and vain and thinks everyone wants to date him.

SQUEAKY AND SQUIRMY

Affiliation: Villain Kids (VKs)

Home Kingdom: Isle of the Lost

SQUEAKY AND SQUIRMY'S RELATIONSHIPS

Twin brothers

Sons of Smee

Along with Celia and Dizzy, Squeaky and Squirmy were in the second group of VKs to join Auradon Prep. They are quiet and shy but are interested in chess, marching band, and debate club at school.

They love the ocean and fishing with their father.

Smee

SMEE

Home Kingdom: Isle of the Lost

SMEE'S RELATIONSHIPS

Father of Squeaky and Squirmy

Smee is a bosun and pirate. He was Captain Hook's first mate on the *Jolly Roger* before being exiled to the Isle of the Lost. Despite working alongside Captain Hook, Smee never fully embraced his villainous ways. Instead, he was more concerned with keeping the peace on Captain Hook's ship. Now that his pirating career is over, Smee enjoys spending time with his sons and teaching them to fish.

Squeaky

Squirmy

MORGIE

Affiliation: Villain Kid (VK)
Home Kingdom: Isle of the Lost

MORGIE'S RELATIONSHIPS

Son of Morgana le Fay

Morgie was part of the VK clique at Merlin Academy, along with Uliana, Hook, Hades, and Maleficent. Morgie desperately wanted Uliana to like and respect him. He was quick to compliment her and would do whatever she said. He could also be dense and wasn't the best liked in the group.

Morgana le Fay

MORGANA LE FAY

Home Kingdom: Isle of the Lost

MORGANA LE FAY'S RELATIONSHIPS

Mother of Morgie

Morgana le Fay is a powerful dark sorceress. She studied with Merlin before turning on him and becoming his enemy. She is cruel and merciless and feels no guilt about hurting innocent people to achieve more power.

Morgie

GIL

Affiliation: Villain Kid (VK)
Home Kingdom: Isle of the Lost

GIL'S RELATIONSHIPS

Son of Gaston

Gil is a VK and part of Uma's band of pirates on the Isle of the Lost. While not the most academic VK on the Isle, he's loyal to his friends and is definitely thehappiest and goofiest of the VKs. He has ended up befriending the VKs who were originally his enemies and is especially close to Jay. They have tentative plans to travel around Auradon to see all the things they missed while growing up on the Isle.

G

Gaston

GASTON

Home Kingdom: Isle of the Lost

GASTON'S RELATIONSHIPS

Father of Gil

Gaston is an arrogant and closed-minded person. Before being sent to the Isle of the Lost, Gaston tried to convince Belle to marry him, even though he didn't understand or appreciate her at all. He was cruel to Belle's father and called the townspeople to kill Beast while Beast was still cursed.

Gil

The Queen of Hearts
Red
The Mad Hatter
Maddox Hatter
Beast — Belle
Maleficent — Hades
Ben
Mal
Gaston
Gil
Lady Tremaine
Anastasia
Drizella
Cinderella — King Charming
Dizzy
Chad
Chloe
Fairy Godmother
Cruella
Jane
Carlos and Dude
Jafar
Jay
Uliana and Ursula
Uma
Aladdin — Jasmine
Family